The Magic of Letters

The Magic *of* Letters

Tony Johnston and Wendell Minor

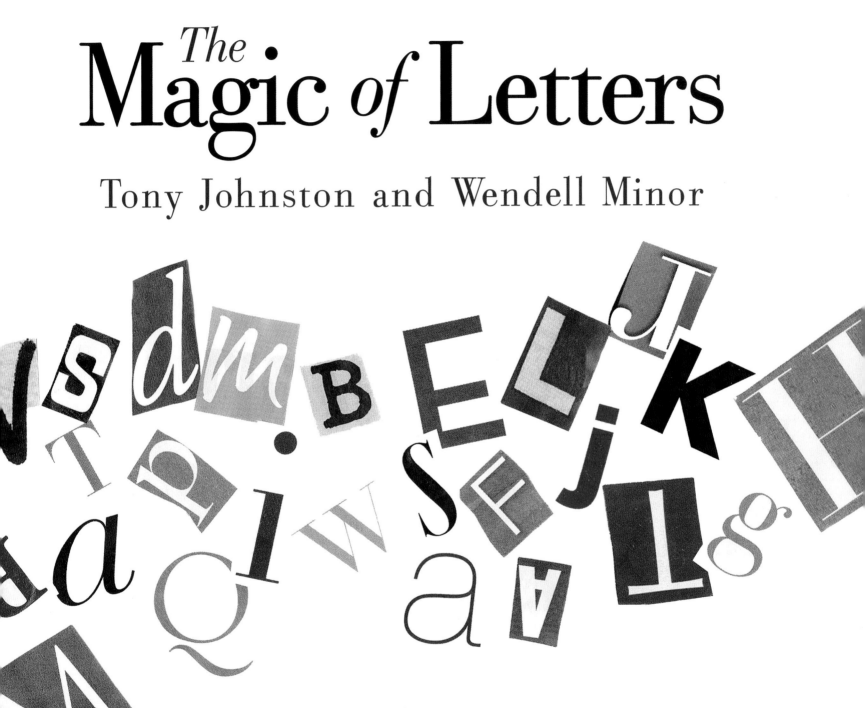

NEAL PORTER BOOKS

HOLIDAY HOUSE / NEW YORK

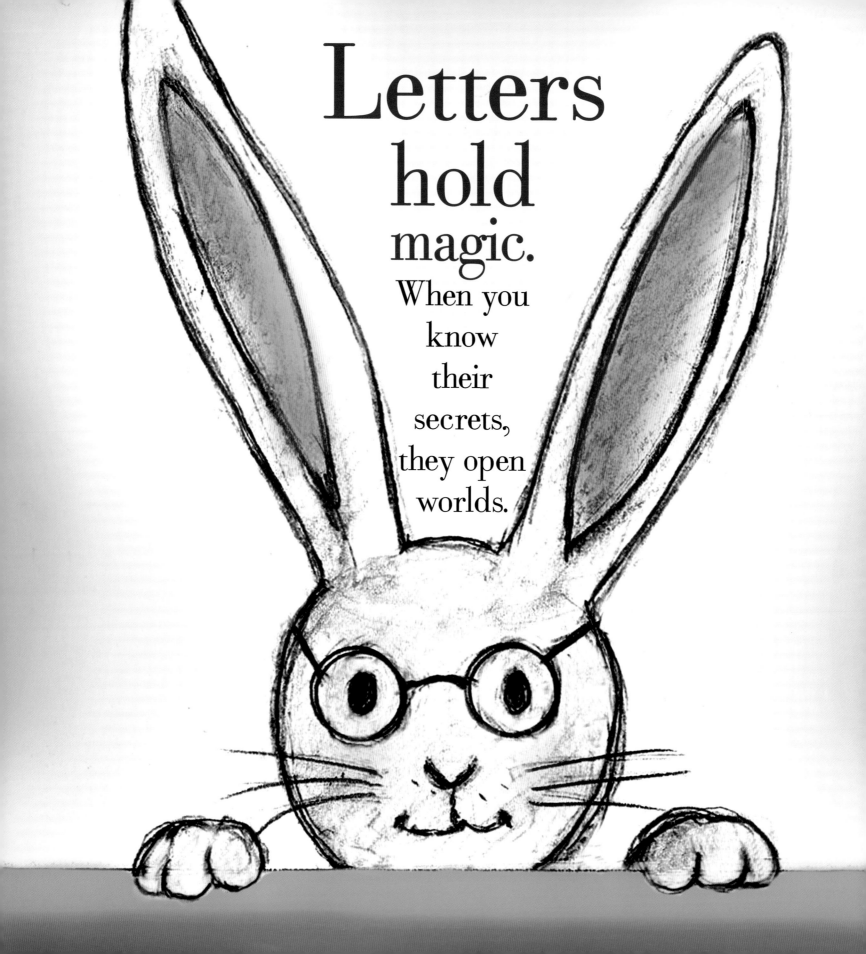

Letters
hold
magic.
When you
know
their
secrets,
they open
worlds.

Each letter has a name, wonderful and strange.

Say each name until
it is your friend.
Then form each
letter, again, again.
When you place
them just so, they say—
your name.

Noah Isaac

otte Elijah Lily Gray

Benjamin Asha Min Carter

Madison Logan Chloe Hiroshi

Ryan Aaliyah Luke Avery Dan

liam **Maria** Gabriel Scarlette Ari

yce Noor Isaac Addison Sebastian

Mateo Cameron Leah Wyatt Eli

Nathan Trang Ahmad Nichola

zie Julian Peyton Elle Mari

Grace Isiah Flo

Letters hold
POWER.

You can shuffle them
around to make loads
of mighty words.

Limber words like acrobat.

Thumpy words like **clunk.**

Slippery words like *trout.*

Giggling
words
like

flibberti

gibbet.

Yummy words like

QUES

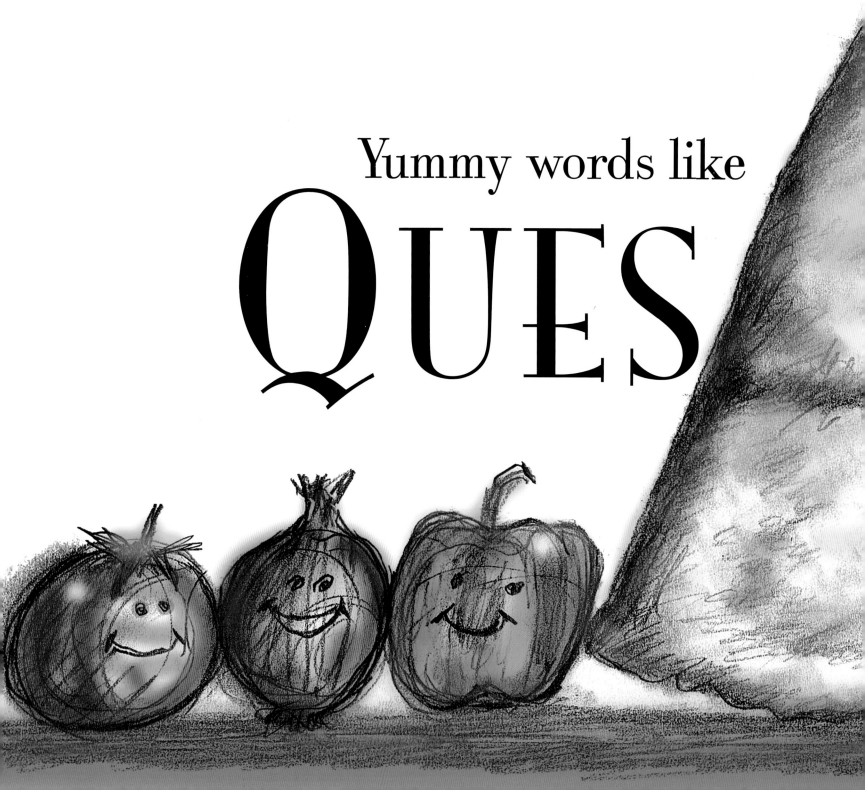

DILLA.

Bewitching words like

enchanted.

Roll them in
your mouth like
lollipops.

Clunk. *Acrobat.*

Trout. QUESADILLA.

Flibbertigibbet.

You will
be *enchanted.*

Now string them together until they say what you need to tell somebody.

The flibbertigibbet ate an enchanted quesadilla

and
became
an acrobat,
who slipped
on a trout—

clunk!

Letters hold
surprises.
If you swinkle
them sweetly,

new words
appear—
like swinkle.

The more words you know,
the more magic
pours out.

Carrots
love

dirt.

You
can write
that.

or—

That cat
fears
the hat.

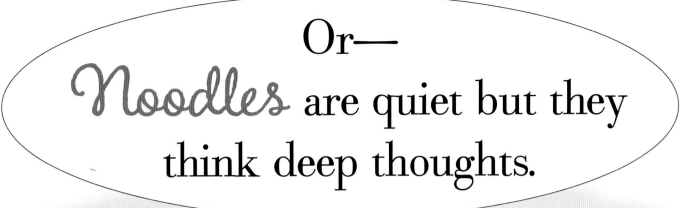

Or—
Noodles are quiet but they think deep thoughts.

Or—
I love
my brother
—or sister—
a lot.

Letters hold magic.
When you know
their secrets,
like a bright
bird,
you take
flight.

You can **read**,
to discover anything
you want.

You can **write**,
everything that
is in your head,
everything that
is in your **heart**.

For my grandson, Noah,
who on the first day of kindergarten said,
"We're learning the letters, but what do they do?"—T. J.

To all children who discover the magic of reading —W. M.

Neal Porter Books

Text copyright © 2019 by The Johnston Family Trust

Illustrations copyright © 2019 by Wendell Minor

All Rights Reserved

HOLIDAY HOUSE is registered in the U.S. Patent and Trademark Office.

Printed and Bound in July 2018 at Toppan Leefung, Dong Guan City, China.

The artwork was created with graphite on paper and digital tools.

www.holidayhouse.com

First Edition

1 3 5 7 9 10 8 6 4 2

Library of Congress Cataloging-in-Publication Data

Names: Johnston, Tony, 1942- author. | Minor, Wendell, illustrator.

Title: The magic of letters / Tony Johnston and Wendell Minor.

Description: First edition. | New York : Neal Porter Books, Holiday House,

[2019] | Summary: Illustrations and easy-to-read text reveal the secrets

of letters, including their power to create words of all kinds.

Identifiers: LCCN 2018009007 | ISBN 9780823441594 (hardcover)

Subjects: | CYAC: Alphabet—Fiction. | Vocabulary—Fiction.

Classification: LCC PZ7.J6478 Mag 2019 | DDC [E]—dc23

LC record available at https://lccn.loc.gov/2018009007